Copyright © 2001 by Paul Stickland
All rights reserved
Published in 2001 in the United States by Ragged Bears
413 Sixth Avenue, Brooklyn, New York 11215
www.raggedbears.com

Simultaneously published in Great Britain by Ragged Bears
Milborne Wick, Sherborne, Dorset DT9 4PW

CIP Data is available

First American Edition
Printed in China
ISBN: 1-929927-34-7
2 4 6 8 10 9 7 5 3 1

BEARS!

PAUL STICKLAND

RAGGED BEARS

BROOKLYN, NEW YORK • MILBORNE WICK, DORSET

I lay in bed with all my toys,
I thought I heard a *furry* noise...

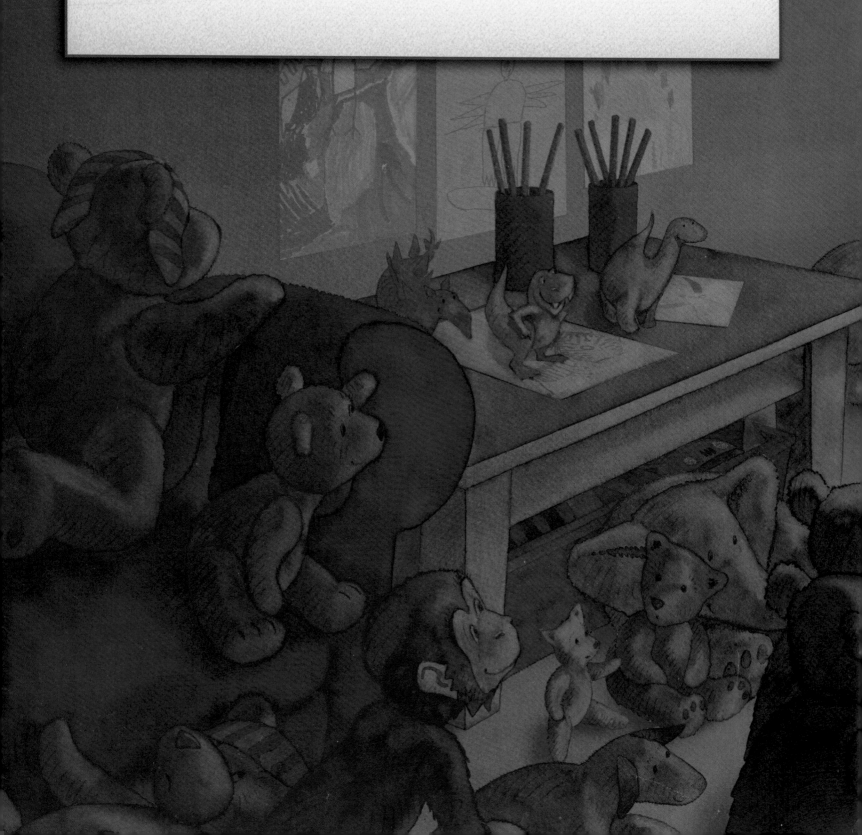

I peered around my bedroom door,
My eyes grew wide with what I saw:

In the hall down by the stairs,
Were lots of very cuddly bears.

It seemed a party had begun,
And everyone was having fun,
I wasn't scared, I couldn't be,
The bears were friendly as could be!

At first there were just one or two,
But then their numbers grew and grew,
Until you really couldn't hide
From bears who now were here, inside!

I wondered whether Mommy knew,
She'd figure out just what to do.
I couldn't even see the stairs,
There simply were too many bears!

I thought I'd better tell my Dad
About the problem that we had.
I asked those bears to move aside,
Dashed to the bedroom, ran inside.

They rested there in deepest sleep,
But I had news I couldn't keep.
So up I jumped and gave a shake,
And *pretty* soon they were awake.

But they didn't seem to worry
That things had gotten wild and furry.
"Come on, come on and look downstairs,
It's absolutely full of bears!"

So Dad got up and shouted, "SHOO!"
And I went out and I looked too,
But all those bears had simply gone,
Except for just one special one.

I climbed in bed
    and tried to sleep...
        ...I thought I heard
            the sound of...

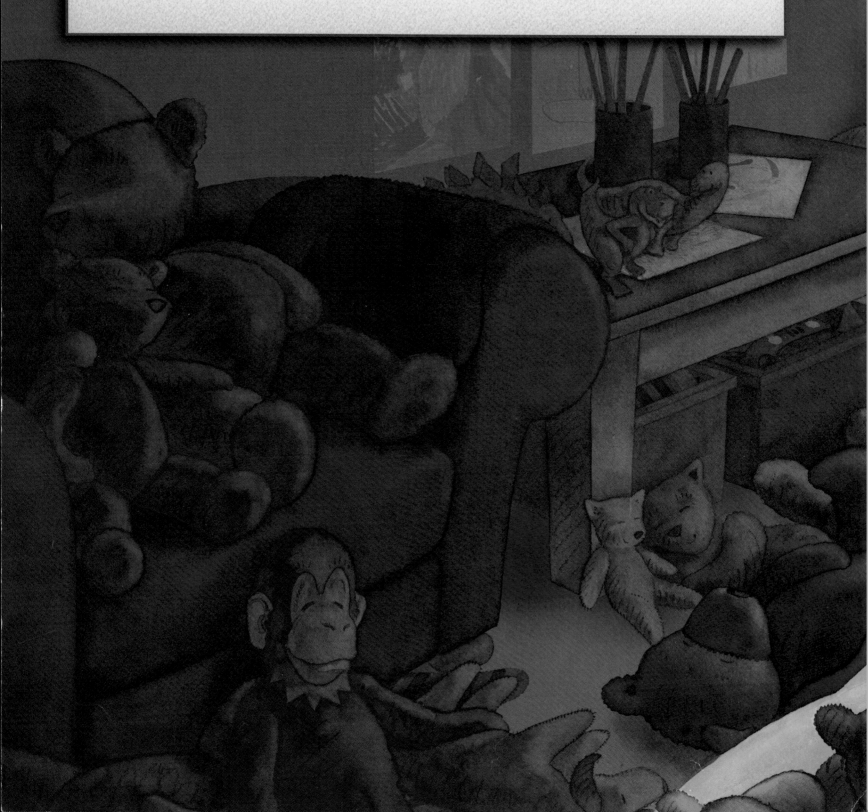

...*sheep!*